MOONLIGHT

SHADES OF LIGHTNING

ADITYA JATKAR

For my parents, who dealt with me.

For Surekha and Shobha Aaji, who grew me up.

For Rishi, Hari, Ishaan and Vishesh, who gave me a place.

Author's Note

To begin with a show of gratitude, the foremost of which is extended to every one of my English professors, who cultivated within me the love of language and the passion to explore the limits to which creativity can be stretched. My friends, who taught me the importance a smile can hold in grave times. Thank you to Simran, Tanayaa and Priyanshi for educating me about female fashion, despite my absolute ignorance towards that entire field. To my Aai and Baba who never once doubted my dreams, jumbled as they were within one another.

If the words laid upon the pages ahead are of any meaning, then it is that if you love, then love deeply, love loudly and clutch firmly onto the bonds of love with every ounce of force you can produce.

Love fully and grieve terribly. Open your heart.

Give them a call once in a while.

New Moon

Summer came quickly in the East. A hot summer wind, riding high like a wave, sweeping across the countryside, cutting the night short to a mere stump of what felt like far too long of an ebony darkness through winter. Snow melted akin to a soft, white downpour, parting away from their companions in the shingles they rested upon, gazing upon countless nights of great frost, only to separate by the coming of a long-awaited dawn, revealing a long-hidden sheet of crimson.

By early May, the ice broke, touched by gold, allowing for all manner of fauna to wind their way across the once petrified river once more. The summer wind blows in an air of refreshment. Dwellers in their holes of comfort, burrow out. Sons, daughters, pushed out into the waves of youth by mothers, fathers, who find themselves lost in their own conquests of survival and stoicism. Conquests under revealed shingles and on broken cobble paths carried on the warmth of a sun that shone ever so brightly with the leave of winter. Near great trees of old that held many tales, unfinished, many meetings, bitter and many lovers, cascading on paths straying further from each other every day, unbeknownst under the veil of convenient bliss. Across great lakes, that held many a reflection of hope and futility and those of many daunting moons that held captive the fates of one too many kindred spirits.

It was at the behest of this summer breeze that the town of Kenterbury sprang into tides of great bustle, swathes of youngsters moving about, seeking to grow out of their shells and prove themselves to the great expanse. Nestled within a relatively quiet corner of the town, was a cottage, plain in sight and a little towards the smaller end as far as cottage hierarchies were concerned. Here too, were the divorced shingles, laid bare under the summer sun. Quiet shingles, quiet chimney, quiet smoke and a quiet home. Residing within this home at present was in fact one of the kindred souls who would soon be swept away on the breeze of youth, not vastly different from the native spring dandelions of Kenterbury, a delicate flower that bloomed in abundance near this quiet home of the kindred soul we speak about. At the tender age of 17, William Eisenhardt had grown into the frame of a rather dapper young man, sporting a bush of ruffled black hair, wild and free, atop his head and adorned with eyes that many enthusiastic admirers had compared to shimmering emeralds. The boy was blessed with a coat of light bronze skin, which glistened in the summer rays, complemented by a tight, muscular build that he had developed over years of particularly rough work with his father. William now remained as one of two inhabitants of the quiet cottage, aptly dubbed 'The Greet of Silence', a product of its long years of solace within the quiet corners of Kenterbury. The Greet was home to William and his father, and was gradually turning towards just his father, as the boy stayed away from home as though it cast a great plague upon his being upon its very sight. This was, of course, far from the truth. William bore no hatred for his ancestral home, humble as it was, and stayed away as a product of circumstance, as was expected of a boy his age. A boy with great ambition. Great courage. Great love even.

Incidentally, it so happened that in the years past, a great fever of exploration and adventure had taken grasp over the youth of Kenterbury, following a grand showing during the annual Winterfest of two summers ago, where messengers of the Capital had put on full display the Crown Regencies plans of constructing the Eastward Ships and the carrying forth towards the Valda expedition, a great journey towards the unexplored lands and continents that lay to the east of Arendor, the vast Crownlands, the southern bowels of which within, lay Kenterbury. In the time of three summers, a marvellous fleet of great ships would be built in the harbour of Kenterbury itself, calling for an assembly of the land's greatest shipwrights, sailors and adventurers, who would venture beyond east of what was east, towards lands yet unmapped. The prospect of foreign glory had ignited the hearts of many, young and old, who sought great rewards from the Crowns expedition. This flame burned bright in William, who held great expectations of adventure and conquest in unknown lands and wished for only one reward, that which pertaineth to simply setting sights on these dramatic landscapes they were promised through the idea of the Eastward Ships. And so, every day, the boy set out, deep within the woods, a hefty pack of books and volumes by his side, in pursuit of knowledge regarding everything involving the building of these great ships, and all that was known of the eastward lands of Valda, which was scarce little.

It was so that William stayed far from home, and so, stayed far away from his father, Erik Eisenhardt. A gruff man, with a strong degree of clarity regarding the way he wished to lead his life. Erik came from the long line of Eisenhardt stonemasons, distant relatives of whom once worked directly under the Crown Regent in the Capital. A humble life had found the Eisenhardt family, and brought them to the Greet, where they had established a content living that served them well for 170 summers now and 34 winters. Erik Eisenhardt embraced this manner of existence and took great pride within his ancestral craft, to which extent, the Eisenhardt line had become the most prominent family of stonemasons in a part of the Westerlands where skills related to the working of many intricate stone works and gems was in were in exceptional demand. Despite obtaining what many would call a seat of fame, Erik continued through with the deferential life placed upon his family from ages past. In a manner of misfortune, however, the years had been far from kind towards the aged stonemason, as was observant through his every action and conduct towards his trade within recent times, a matter that was beginning to grow of considerable concern to his young child, who worried greatly for his father, whom he deeply loved and held great admiration for. The relations between the two had always been a beautiful bond of father and son, although perhaps to an outsider's eye, it would not seem so, given that Erik was a particularly gruff man, exceptionally skilled at his craft, but ever so slightly intimidating to be around. It was a matter of great tragedy and an event that shaped the lives of both father and son, when Erik's wife passed to sickness 15 winters ago, when William was only 2, leaving him to fend for his son on his lonesome, while steeped in grief at the loss of his love. It was despite the extensive efforts of every mage and healer's aid that she succumbed to a grave illness that seemed nigh incurable, a fact that still did not diminish Erik's hope till her last day, after which he crumbled into a deep depression. It was in those months that the fires of the Eisenhardt forge ran colder than permafrost. Over the passing of many summers though, Erik returned to his craft, if only to ensure that William was not made a victim of his grief. At the age of only 11, the boy adopted a keen affluency of skills within the forge, much to his father's surprise who had begun his journey as a stonemason at 19, after years of very demanding training, as was required by Eisenhardt tradition, long after they settled in Kenterbury, and long before even, when they worked in service of the Crown. Perhaps Erik would have provided the boy with the proper training, but after his mother's death his concern remained solely with giving him every quantity of love and affection he would never receive from her. And so, even when despite his skill at the forge, William often strayed away towards prospects of adventure and wonder, much like his mother who herself was a renowned explorer and one who took great interest in simply the idea of Valda, Erik never questioned it and neither did he stop him, pushing past any scepticism, or wish for his son to stay by his side, for he would give any and all for him.

The Eisenhardt pair worked their way across Kenterbury across many fronts, with William serving as apprentice for the town's Acting Head of Mystical Exploration, Syrion Cray, a man of considerable eccentrics when it came to his occupation and also a man who was an object of particular disdain for Erik, taking into consideration his distinctively gruff nature, which served as a stark contrast towards Cray, very poorly aided by the fact that his beloved son and heir was, well in the eyes of Erik, 'bludgeoned by the blind guidance of a shipwright who couldn't tell his ass from his mouth'. The colourful language utilised by Mr Eisenhardt, often brought the two to odds, the product of which resulted in an unfortunately heavy storm of burdens upon young William. Despite these squabbles, the Eisenhardts held a deep familial bond, and despite these fair few misgivings about the true value of what his son strove to achieve through his dedication towards the journey East, his love for his only son forbade him from ever placing a shackle on his desires, as he greatly admired the man he had become and wished for his good fortune as a doting father.

It was in those early days of summer, that William set forth, within the silent hues of the morning, to a resplendent Kenterbury, painted in the sharp onset of a rising dawn, as he made his way to the Magistrate of Foreign Affairs, where Cray took office and conducted any and all affairs of pertinence to the expedition East. When bathed in gold, courtesy of the morns early twilight hours, the Magistrate was a rather magnificent building, taking a great degree of pride as it stood tall and upright within the very heart of the town, at four stories tall, fashioned from the fragrant mahogany, found exclusively within the Crownlands to the north, and adorned with a stardome of breathtaking beauty, described by Cray as a crystal gate separating the realms of heaven and earth, quite in line with his usual descriptions of grandeur regarding most of everything within the world, and most of all, any and all things in relation to the Eastward Ships, and the prospect of Valda.

In days past, prior to the great Winterfest of two summers ago, the Magistrate was, well in comparison to its grand state as of the day William approached it, a construction that many would consider slightly unsightly, accredited towards the long history of neglect in regards to matters pertaining to the school of terms that were placed under the word 'foreign'. The south of Arendor was a region below the Crownlands, titled Erfenia, divided into four regions of not greatly distinct nature, but distant enough to be classified as lands of separated peoples and cultures. These lands were then named Inarion to the West, Fae Gyora towards the South, The Glades to the East and Erenheldor towards the North, sister to the Crownlands. It was to the far east of the Glades, which many southlanders termed as east of east, that Kenterbury lay, a port city to the Gulf of Vedrinoldr, termed within legend as the remains of a great and terrifying battle between ancient gods of sea and storm. The people of the Glades, and of course, Kenterbury, had over the vast prospect of time, come to grow greatly content of their dwellings within the peaceful bay, embracing the many summers and winters they had met with over the years, and it was a beautiful life indeed, where the populace of the town grew through a shared history of familial bonds of friendship and fostered a deep care towards the land and their fellow kinsmen, and blossomed into specialists within a great many crafts, trade with the Crownlands through means of business transactions chief among them, serving as a pillar towards Kenterbury's economic standing within Erfenia. It became so, that the prospect of foreign exploration and the idea of conquest to feast on promised riches and treasures, appeared to be one of a seemingly unprofitable future, as the inhabitants of the Glades and the Southlands as a whole appeared more than satisfied within the means they were granted to lead their living.

However, this had not seemed to be the case within the Crownlands. For a great many years now, the royal lineage had been in a progressive state of decay, since the passing of the great King Surton, First of his name and wielder of the Crimson Blade of Imladrion, the deity of fire within the Arendorian mythos. By use of the blazing strength of the ancient Lord of Fires and Ashes, Surton had by sweeping success, suppressed countless rebellions from the North of Arendor, titled Rykaria, a fractured land of many who would place upon themselves the title of lord, commanders of their own sects, through a series of meagre claims and treacherous overthrowings. Long had the men of this land, coveted the high seat of the Arendorian King, laying within the capital city of Arianor, held among the great fields and valleys of the Crownlands, to no avail however, as the royal lineage had for an age, held them at bay through the collective strength of the Crown and with aid from the peoples of Erfenia, alongside a great many mystical powers, derived as relics from the Gods of that land.

But it was within the time of 122 summers past, when ill tidings befell the Crownlands, as the realm was made aware of Surton's passing to the grievous illness he had contracted as a result of a deep wound suffered during a great battle led by him against the Craven Frostlord of Holfingr, within Holfinarön, who had launched a barrage of ice magic in his cowardice against the Arianorian host, striking the valiant king during his charge against the men of that land to stave off their skirmishes towards the Crownlands. Despite a furious campaign, which resulted in the utter decimation of the Frostlord and his lands, within the unrelenting inferno of Imladrion, the High King was unable to recover from the wounds suffered by him in the midst of battle, as these wounds of his were a product of magical infusion of northern ice magic, a cold and brutal form of sorcery, designed to inflict the victim with a cold, slow and painful end. Following Surton's tragic yet unexpected death, the reigns of the Crown and the royal lineage passed into the hands of his descendants, who served as mere shadows of their predecessors, as a lack of control, ineffectiveness and inexperience shone like a harsh light towards their subjects, causing unrest within the people and an ever growing threat from the North, who recounted and regathered their forces following the loss of the Frostlord and the lands of Holfinarön. It was so, that in the years to come, the seat of the Arianorian King was dissolved and a Ministership was installed to supplement the rule of the royal lineage who now ruled under the title of Crown Regent.

Despite this adjustment to the political workings of the Crown, Arianor would continue to steep itself within the bowels of a slow decay, causing disarray within the kingdom, growing ever further with time. It was near this point, that the eldest amongst those of the Reinstark clan, Viktor Reinstark, titled The Chisel, as a sign of great respect to his skill as a renowned stonemason and leader of that clan who were chief blacksmiths and stonemasons to the crown, took it upon himself to move apart and away from all workings of the monarchy, given their failing system that seemed to grow ever worse in those years past. However, not all people of the Reinstarks aligned in order to the views of The Chisel, placing their faith in the hope of revitalisation, which was all but lost, seeing as the heirs of Surton were utterly incompetent, and above all, unable to harness the Crimson Blade, which faded into a tale of myth, although legend dictates that it returned to the hands of Imladrion himself, by whose decree it would pass only to one with the strength to bear the inferno, however, none of such calibre would rise within the royal lineage again. And so, Viktor led those of his kin who wished to follow his ideal, south towards The Glades of Erfenia, in hopes of finding a content living, free of the shortcomings that the Crown could not cease to produce, within a then humble village that would soon grow to be a bustling port, known as Kenterbury, creating a quiet keep for himself known in very many years to come as 'The Greet of Silence' and took the name 'Eisenhardt', which would then pass on to the great line of stonemasons that would eventually produce Erik and William Eisenhardt.

Looking back to the events of two summers past, whence the Magistrate of Foreign Affairs lay in a fairly sorry state, while this was the general attitude towards matters of foreign exploration within Kenterbury then, the Crown, in fact, had been conducting no few number of expeditions of their own towards Valda, in the hope of claiming resources and treasures that could aid what had now become an utter structural and economic failure within the Crownlands, a product of the long decay suffered to the governance of the land, following Surton's passing, now ruled by the current Crown Regent, Gordolfen the Glutton, a disappointment to the lineage on almost every front. The announcement of the building of the Eastward Ships at the Winterfest of two summers ago in Kenterbury, had been a technique employed by the collective collaboration of the Crown and the Ministership, in order to bolster the numbers of 'explorers' sent to Valda, in an attempt to syphon the lands riches and wealth, which was now observed by Arianor as the last hope of revitalisation and a means to stave off the clans of Rykaria. The prospect of the Eastward Ships and Valda, worked to great effect, mostly amongst the young, blooming populace of Kenterbury, who viewed the journey and the adventure to follow as rewards of treasure and glory, seemingly akin to a dream, to those young kindreds who were grown on the tales of Surton's glory and the tumultuous deeds of kings and heroes past.

Following the public support of the journey East expressed by the monarchy and the governors of the capital, the Magistrate, which had long stayed under a veil of general unimportance within Kenterbury, was spruced up to be the monumental attraction of the town that it stood as in present day, and served also, as the office of William's mentor, Syrion Cray, an agent of the capital who was placed to ensure the smooth construction and journey of the Eastward Ships towards Valda.

It was on that day, that in the first shades of the morning, as William stepped within that grand keep of all manner of mystics and foreign knowledge, that he was met with the distinctively loud welcome of his master and mentor, Cray. Nestled within an array of tattered scrolls and parchments high above the woodworks of the initial floor, William caught sight of that man of great enthusiasm from a ways away, simply through the shine of his robes, which carried a deep violet hue, sewn in with the royal gold of the capital, as his hands were weighed down by a great many adornments and rings of arcane origin. He wore his hair, salt and pepper in shade, slicked back, with the passing of many years visible on his face as he turned towards his student. His voice was heavy, deep but clear, his tone however, often dissipated the seriousness that was usually coupled with a voice of that vocal depth as he let out a rather high pitched welcome - "William! My boy, my dear boy! So you have come, within this hour of shining shades amongst the early summer sky. Come dear boy, sit. There is much to unravel amongst us, master and student". The young Eisenhardt had grown accustomed to his teacher's passionate expression of himself and responded in a kind respect to his peer, who he admired very much in light of his own passions and vigour to explore the East and the journey therefore.

"Master! It pleases me to see you in such high spirits, and indeed, I have arrived in every hope to converse within your vast wisdom on this day that welcomes the dawn of this new sun." said William, eager to discuss where his mentor would next guide him further regarding their joint work towards the expedition. The pair had joined as student and master a summer past, with Cray facilitating William's innate love to reach beyond the shores of Arendor, through his teachings of the great mysticisms and treasures that lay East. In his knowledge, which was passed onto him from the findings of Arianor's journeys to Valda, he illuminated the boy upon the sights and wonders of that land. Within the late hours, in flickering lamplight, master and student would learn together of great mountains of fire, forests of magical charms and wastes of endless heat and chalk within the East. As apprentice to the master of the Eastward Ships within Kenterbury, through the year past, William had spent most of his time under the wise elder, learning not only of the tales and records of Valda, but also of the craft of the shipwrights and the intricacies of that perilous journey that he wished to one day undertake. Cray had imparted upon him this great knowledge, alongside delegating certain errands of minor inconvenience to the boy, mostly involving the collection of certain materials for his studies or the construction of minor devices that would eventually be used in some part of the great journey, thus leaving William without a great degree of substantial work to his name as Cray's apprentice, despite accumulating a vast hoard of knowledge from the man, which, certainly kindled a roaring passion within the young Eisenhardt regarding the travels and prospects of the East, yet leaving him without the opportunity to make any significant contribution to Cray's efforts thus far.

It was so on this first day of the new summer that William approached his mentor with a long sown desire that had been festering within him since Cray's promise to him, made within the fading months of the previous year, crafting words most compelling to tell William that by the coming of next summer, the boy would be granted a task of utmost importance to aid with the journey East, one that would certainly cement his name within the great captains of that voyage who led their people to lands of magic and riches unknown.

Within Cray's mind was every knowledge of his young student's longing for the permission to accomplish this feat and from high above the great shelves of scrolls and parchments of the Magistrate did he look down upon him, ready now, to grant him this privilege. But it would come to pass that perhaps this journey was not quite a gift, and the true value it would present remained yet veiled. This fact however remained unknown to both student and master. So he began, as William entered the inner chambers of the Magistrate where the two had now drifted. "How do you fare of late, dear boy. It has been quite a while since we last sat, student and master together, within those fading hours of the long nights before the coming of this new summer." His voice rang clear and deep. Now separated from his general enthusiasm, yet not lacking care and control as he sat within his seat at the centre of the Magistrate, within its innermost chamber, illuminated by a vast skylight to his back, which filtered in the colours of the early dawn that had now grown brighter in the wake of the sun. "The days have been met only with eagerness Master. Every passing week has been a measure of my patience, for summer could not have come ever quicker. You know of my longings, to prove my worth, Master!" said William, hasty now after long days of limbo before the coming of summer. The sunlight broke through the warm shades of dawn, illuminating the boy's face at whom Cray looked towards, in a certain sense of admiration, taking pride in what his student had grown into the past year. "Indeed dear boy", said Cray, coating his words with a sense of reassurance towards the eager youth "As I had made this promise to you before the coming of summer, I now intend to fulfil it to its complete extent. Now, listen closely". And in those hours of the bright summer sun did Cray begin unravelling his plans for his apprentice, aligned with the coming of the new season.

"I had indeed told you that by this first day of the new moon and the beginning of the sun's dominance over our lands, you, William, would be allowed to accomplish a task of great significance to the journey East," said Cray "And so, now that we have worked in unison for a year, master and student together, I bestow upon you this great opportunity. Within these long years past, the expeditions to the land of Valda have all been conducted from the capital, but never once from lands of the south, and the path which we tread towards those lands, eastward bound, leads to a sect of the continent that remains yet undiscovered, and so we have little knowledge of where our journey makes landfall. Since at present we face this lack of geographical knowledge dear boy, we are in dire need of a tool used to chart our path, a wayfinder, so to speak." Upon this, William was eager to interject, as the boy was a craftsman now of no ignorable measure, to whom the creation of a wayfinder, a common tool utilised by explorers within those lands, would be a task of relative ease, however this notion of assumption was quickly cut short by his master, almost as if Cray had a window to peek into his thoughts, rapid as they flowed through each passing minute. "Now boy, I know that the crafting of a wayfinder would appear not further than the task of a child to a master of the crafts such as you," said Cray, however his student was firm to clutch his modesty as he spoke "The ease of the task is a matter of little concern to me Master. The sway it would bring about towards aiding our great journey comes first to me". Yet again, Cray was impressed by the devout nature of his student, as the young Eisenhardt had mastered himself when it came to his conduct towards his master and his tasks.

"Then it would please you to understand that this task presents itself as quite the challenge, my dear apprentice. For I ask of you to craft not a wayfinder of ordinary make. You see, to complete a journey towards the lands of the East, or in this case rather, to chart the path, we require a rather special device." It was at this point that William felt an intriguing mixture of excitement and confusion. "Let this be the latest of the lessons I impart to you William, of those mystical lands that lay beyond the reach of most men and beasts alike. The path across from the vast seas of Belehrad is treacherous, and to navigate them, we require an ancient piece of technology, from those times lost, when gods and deities still roamed the land, called the Vedrivisir. It is a device of mystical power that channels through it the strengths and remnants of those beings who once fought within the waters of this land and created Vedrinoldr. Within that great gulf lay the Stormjewel Isles, what many call the remains of that great battle. It is there my boy, that you will find the components required to craft this legendary artefact. But the journey serves has a testament to your skill Eisenhardt, as those lands are perilous indeed, and yet harbour the fury of the old gods, which is why it is all the more necessary for you to gain those pieces of the Vedrivisir which syphon that ancient power, necessary to navigate the seas to our destination." And upon hearing these words, William found it difficult to mask his joy, however the boy maintained his composure when faced by his Master. "The task you have set before me, Master, is one of great challenge and endurance. I need not say the great honour you have bestowed upon me by allowing me to aid the journey East in a manner of such paramount importance. Thank you Master."

Within that chamber, flooded by sunlight, William took a knee before the elderly Minister, in a show of respect to the man whom he had apprenticed under and now granted him a wondrous opportunity to prove his merit as one who dreamed of traversing the vast lands beyond his home, that lay yet uncharted.

"Rise, dear boy. You have made no little show of your worth as one who would travel with us to what lies East of East. Well I suppose, in this case it would be East of East of East." he chuckled for a brief second, before ceasing after he was met with a rather cold silence from his apprentice. The boy had never quite gotten a grasp towards appreciating humour. That, coupled with Cray's usual eccentrics falling into generally subpar categories of comedy. "Uh, yes. Regardless of your valour and courage as one so young, it remains that the journey is indeed perilous and not lacking in troubles on the road. Therefore, you will undertake this task with a partner." The silence that followed was brief, but this time it was more in line with strong notions of confusion coming from William. "But Master, I was of the thought that this was an honour granted to me alone, a reward for the work we have accomplished in the year past. Why is it that I need a supplement to this journey?" questioned the boy, disheartened only in the slightest. "William, you must understand the risk you take under the name of this honour. It is not one to be slighted nor ignored, and in my good conscience, I must reduce the risk of harm to you in every manner that matters, lest I also face the wrath of your father, considering our relations are not quite far from sour at the moment, dear boy. This is still your journey. Your task. But deny not the aid boy, for it comes not of any ill to you." Master and student lay parallel to each other, and while William was now steeped in questions, doubts rather, it would serve him little purpose to voice them. He would play the card he was dealt, for the path ahead lay with yet another chance to display his worth. Regardless of the means through which it would be achieved. "I accept it, Master. My apologies for speaking against it. I will undertake the journey through any and all means deemed necessary by you." Of course, despite this statement, the boy yet harboured no small number of hesitations regarding the information that was revealed to him. It was his choice, however, to place them aside, quite aligned with the nature of most Eisenhardt, working in order to finish any task at hand, not quite concerned with the elements involved.

"It is in the hours of the night that I want you to travel to the Lake of Zephyr. Meet the one who would accompany you within the slopes of that land. I believe the journey ahead would require no small amount of discussion regarding the manner in which you would go about it. Approach it with no trace of a closed mind my boy. Keep to yourself that it is a necessity. Now come. We study till nightfall. It would serve you well to learn more of the Vedrivisir, and the many pitfalls hidden within the Vedrinoldr." No further discussions were made of the matter regarding William's partner and the pair continued on, passing once again to the upper sections of the Magistrate, where enveloped within woodworks and pieces of generational knowledge, William was told about the long histories of Kenterbury, and that which led to the forming of the Vedrinoldr alongside other tales of ancient times, in relation to the use of the Vedrivisir, which was in fact a device that supposedly used the remnants of the power scattered across the Vedrinoldr through the titanic battles fought in that region between oceanic deities of legend, to navigate across the vast waters through mystical means, following the formation of the device, which in form, appeared not too far from a compass.

It was so that these lessons carried through into the twilight hours, far as they were, for the sun now held reign over the land for a good portion of each day, making those hours of nightfall akin to a scarcity. At sundown, the boy left, carrying words of goodwill from his master, while taking with him also, doubts of his own, and yet William began on his way to the Lake of Zephyr. The lake lay on the outskirts of Kenterbury, held within the folds of the hills that served as a sort of border to the town. It was by no means a body of water that boasted size of enormous proportions and was quite humble in its right, surrounded by few trees of considerable age and flat grass that stretched across the sides of the lake, towards the beaten path that led to it. That region in particular was named in relation to the wonderful breezes that would very often sweep the land and the lake in tandem. It was often a sight to see the tall grass surrounding the lake, swaying to and fro the wind. It intrigued William however, as to why he was heading to the lake for any matter of regards to the preparation for the journey East. Perhaps it was simply a point of convenience for meeting his partner? It was yet odd, as the lake was close enough to the town to be considered a part of the region geographically speaking, and was yet far enough to make it a slight inconvenience to be used a meeting place for anything that did not pertain to simply sitting by the lake in the moonlight, watching and feeling the winds of that land. William was not one to question it however, taking into consideration that the boy was well aware of Cray's wisdom in these affairs.

The road therefore was dark, silent and absent of any presence of the moon above. The first day of summer brought about a new moon, and therefore a black sky. Devoid of light, devoid of illumination. Leaving one to their own thoughts on empty cobbled roads. And so he thought. In fact he thought very much. He thought about his dreams. He thought about the lake. He thought about his partner. Whom he had not ever seen nor taken any regard of in any day past. He thought about his father. His father who so dearly doted on him. The thought came to him that after his trip to the lake, it would likely bring his father immense joy to see him once again, as their meetings had grown ever shorter in light of the boy's apprenticeship. And he kept thinking on that road to the lake as he grew closer to leaving the town. The winds that night under the new moon were cold, sharp even, as William waded his way through them, clothed with not much more than his pants and tunic, which served as a slightly inadequate defence against the chill. He lugged a satchel upon his shoulder as he approached the lake, carrying within it not more than a couple of fruits, and a leather skin flask, holding in it water, taken from the Magistrate, courtesy of his Master, prior to William's leave.

Deep within the night now, equipped with but one lantern of annoyingly dim light, he arrived at the Lake of Zephyr. The moonless night laid bare before it a lightless pit of water, as the winds blew slower now, allowing for the swathes of grass before William to move in a calming rhythm, as he set his satchel to the floor, by the great oak tree that marked the entrance to the lake. He hung the lamp by his waist and looked out over the waters. It was beautiful. Serene. A little pocket of pearl like loch that was captured by the hills. The breeze blew past the young man as he now waited, with no sign of the partner that Cray had told him to find. And so he sat by the great oak, under the moonless sky, continuing to gaze upon that little lake that lay before him, falling once more into his thoughts, as they grasped onto him, like tendrils in the night, as he pondered over those dreams of lands beyond.

What would it be like, he wondered, to witness forests with no end, chasms leading to the very bottom of the earth, fields of dandelions, an expanse with which the eye could only perceive a fraction of what lay ahead. It wasn't the prospect of riches or treasure that drew him towards the East. It was simply the idea. The chance to chart the uncharted, to see that which had never been seen. The south of Valda was a region that even the envoys of the capital had never yet approached, and by all means, it could very well be some manner of a hellscape, barren even, chalk full of hissing flames and mountains of fire and terror that reached upward to the sky. But it was, quite plainly, the prospect of becoming a witness to that great land, terrible as it may have been, that drove him, and perhaps many others of his like who had found within them a great fire of desire following that fateful winter of two summers past. And so he thought, long and deep of these matters, under the oak, where it seemed as every minute was transformed into some otherworldly hour by that midnight breeze. Clouds passed overhead, as the grass continued to sway, while William lay yet in wait.

It was when the boy was lost entirely in his mind, unfocused on any happenings of that around him, that a faint light approached, rightward from where he was sat, and carrying it was a cloaked figure. Not quite tall of stature, and covered by a thick, grey hood, that seemed to drape over their shoulders and downwards to their feet. Must have been quite wary of the cold, thought William, as his gaze now drifted from looking inwards to the light that steadily approached his own. It drew closer until it was only a few feet away from the oak where he sat, with the one in possession of it yet unknown, tucked away behind the protection of their garb. William stood, lifting his lamp as he approached the figure who lay still now, under the branches of the oak under the void of the night sky, as the breeze blew across both their forms. Skinny, he thought. It wasn't like him to pass judgement, however in light of what seemed to be a slight bitterness towards the notion that he was unworthy of completing this task alone, he was in the least, sceptical of how individual was in any way planning to make a significant contribution to aid him with anything that had to with the Vedrivisir. It was when he drew close to the person in front of him that they lifted their hood. Never had it been a task of any ease to take the young Eisenhardt by surprise, and yet the boy was rather frozen, equated to his embarrassment which struck soon, but of course, not escaping to his face, which although shocked, managed to maintain its composure.

His partner was a girl. A girl with flowing locks of dark gold, and eyes of a faint amber green. It was as if they could glow in the lamplight. She wore a fair face, a little small, but crafted with beauty, holding lips of a light cherry. William realised his gaze had been fixated on the girl for perhaps a concerning amount of time, mostly attributed to the shock or perhaps because he had in an amount of suddenness become ever so slightly tensed. She looked up at him. The scene was one of relative awkwardness, considering William was taller and larger than his newfound partner, forcing the latter to stare upwards at a funny angle towards the former. Then, her face tightened. Her eyes, which took a shape not far removed from those of a doe, grew squinted as it appeared as though she was making an analysis of his face. It wasn't the type of situation where William could initiate some sprawling conversation, as he himself was stood still with his guard broken, considering he had expected a meeting with some pasty teenager, upjumped on misguided dreams of some riches and treasures of the East, who Cray had recruited as some sort of token aid to him. It was far from the delicate beauty who stood before him, staring right back at his dumbfounded expression as she made her own silent judgments of the boy.

"Hello."

What? Had she just spoken? Her voice was as clear as a cold mountain spring. William's mind was far from as clear as a cold mountain spring. "Uh, hello. Good evening." It was an hour past midnight. She said nothing back and continued to stare with a face that felt like a labyrinth now. He was unable to decipher her thoughts in the slightest, however, she spoke once more. "So, you're Master Cray's envoy then, I take it?"

Master? Envoy? Just who was this girl? William's mind grew cloudy. Had it been so that Cray had made any mention of a figure as such at any moment in the past? He doubted it. "I believe we misunderstand each other. I'm not an envoy, I was sent here by-" He paused for a fleeting second, taking into consideration just what kind of Master she referred to when speaking of Cray. "-Master Cray, yes, to find the partner he assigned me as aid to the expedition of the Stormjewel Isles. I take it that you would be the partner in question?".

He had gotten past the initial shock of the girl's daintiness and recalled now why he had made the trip to the lake in the first place, as he recalled now that this girl was in fact paramount towards constructing the Vedrivisr, considering that he yet remained without the real knowledge of how to construct the device of legend. In his passing lessons with Cray, thus far he had learned only that the compass was forged of remains and materials found exclusively within the Stormjewel Isles, the old battlefield of the sea gods. Perhaps his newfound partner was the key to discovering and using said materials.

"Ah. My apologies then. It appears you are no envoy." She said, and William believed then that the misunderstanding had cleared and the two were on the path towards a fruitful relationship that would certainly allow the obtaining of the compass with ease. "You must be my subordinate then." Ah, and in another fleeting second, the misunderstanding erected itself once more. "We seem to be reaching an impasse on multiple fronts, Miss...I would have your name, if you please, and perhaps your understanding towards the fact that we are partners. Not envoys or subordinates to each other." His tone was only slightly pinched by frustration, but the boy was patient enough to observe another response. "Uh, yes. I didn't really mean to speak of each other either. It's really just you. Being a subordinate to me. Quite in line with how this excursion should be carried out really. I'm Ilsa Freyr. You may continue to address me as Miss or Miss Freyr. A sign of respect to your superior of course."

Such hubris, William thought. For a face this beautiful, the mind behind it seemed to be quite deceptive in hiding this...arrogance. "I must make it clear once again. Master Cray was sound of speech when he told me that there was no system of superiors amongst this...alliance, and that holds true even now. Anyways, I cannot spend anymore words trying to convince you otherwise. Shall we head to someplace where we can perhaps plan what exactly it is we seek to find in the Isles?" He spoke now only with determination to complete the task at hand. She stared at him once again. Her locks drifted across her face as the winds of the lake picked up once again. He smelled an amalgamation of strawberries and cherries, aromatic, and emitted from her being. Distraction came easy here.

"Very well. I am still of the complete and sound belief that you should most certainly report to me as your peer for this quest, considering only our stark gaps in knowledge and well, experience, seeing as to how I have been working with Master Cray for two whole summers past now, compared to your one, Mr Eisenhardt." She knew his name? But how? Was this something that Master Cray had discussed with this strange woman? Questions plagued William's mind now. Questions that sprang forth like branches of a great tree, that was the statement that she just made. Two summers past? But Syrion Cray had been Acting Head of Foreign Exploration for only two summers exactly. Surely she hadn't begun work with him the very first day they met.

She walked off now, back on the same path she had come, almost as if the sole reason she even came to the lake was to take a gauge of how useful her 'subordinate' really was, leaving all of his questions unanswered and placing on him only the scent of wintery berries. William realised although, that he hadn't actually asked any of those questions that were quickly turning his mind into a labyrinth. He stared as she stopped now, near the other entrance to the Lake of Zephyr. She turned, only slightly, but enough to unveil the faintest of smiles - "So would you like to plan our next steps or just remain captive to the breeze? Come on Eisenhardt, we have a ways ahead of us."

What did she mean? What did she know? Did her sentences really have to be this enigmatic? Was William just making them more cryptic than they seemed? Perhaps all of the above was true, but he decided that perhaps just walking along seemed to be the way forward towards any hope of forging that compass.

He followed in her steps, illuminating the beaten path ahead with only the lamp that rattled across his waist. He saw not much more beyond her cloak as she stepped carefully down the road that now curved downhill, leading closer to a part of Kenterbury that was almost entirely opposite to the Greet of Silence. Unfamiliar to William, but familiar enough to the point where he felt as though his new partner wasn't luring him to a forest mugging or something of that sort. He caught glimpses of her from moment to moment. She kept turning to see if he was still following and he could only tell ever so slightly, only for their eyes to lock when he saw their vivid green shining behind a curtain of gold. He watched vigilantly as they walked, a few feet apart from each other the entire way, with not a word spoken between the two, besides those that managed to escape from those fleeting glances.

She knew his name. He thought again about how the girl knew his name. In his confusion, bewilderment and slight frustration at her assignment of his position as some sort of subordinate, it had not crossed William's mind to give the girl his name. Yet she knew. It occurred to him that the Eisenhardt were most certainly stonemasons of modest renown within Kenterbury, but that name had surely not spread on William's effort and belonged truly to his father. Yet she knew. It raised further intrigues within his mind as they continued to walk on about what exactly Cray had told her, especially taking into consideration her mention of the claim that she had been working with him for apparently a fair bit longer than William. And thus far Cray had made no mention of her whatsoever.

After a long, silent walk away from the Lake of Zephyr under the moonless night sky, the pair arrived at a tavern on the very outskirts of the town. Ilsa's hood was raised as the pair entered, and found a quiet seat for themselves within the corner of the place, within no small amount of noise rushing around, with a number of drunkards who seemed to be having quite the jolly night, drowned in feasts and mead. They navigated through what was an unsightly maze of men stumbling upon themselves, hobbling from one corner of the bar to another, with many carried upon their friends shoulders, a testament to exactly how inebriated they were. The pair walked past as William was increasingly sceptical of the setting they found themselves in, as he asked "I had assumed a slightly quieter setting as our place of discussing any further plans Miss Freyr. Excuse my pessimism but would we not find it just a little difficult to make *any* plans with a drunkard toppling onto us every other minute?" It was at that moment that a drunkard did in fact almost topple onto the pair, sparing his body but not his drink as William shielded the girl from the brunt of the liquid spilling onto her cloak. It was their fortune that the man who had spilled the drink had already moved on now in a fit of drunken laughter onto his next pint across the table next to the two. Ilsa turned back briefly while moving forward to a William who followed, with his sleeve now drenched in mead, as she gazed and said "Thank you for that, but if this is how you're planning on being at the isles as well, you should know that there's plenty of far more unsavoury things that you really won't have the time to whine about." William scoffed after accepting the mild annoyance that came to him rather quick after that statement as they trudged through spilled mead and food towards the corner of the tavern, "This is far from whini-," "Just follow me and worry about the intricacies of what qualifies as whining later." That interruption provided little room for response unfortunately, as despite his growing irritation he continued to follow, reaching the very corner of the establishment now.

As they were seated, the girl now finally rid herself of the cloak, which had seemed unnecessarily heavy to William since they first met at the lake. She wore a vest of olive green, holding a low collar laced with tightly woven streaks of chiffon towards the edges, holding behind it a white bralette that just so allowed the streaks of gold that drifted from cheeks to fall upon her collarbones that shone elegantly on her fair figure. Perhaps William was being a little too attentive. Her hair fell loose, shining by the candlelight as she looked up at him while placing the coat to the side. Ever so slightly, he noticed the formations of a little smirk as she said "We've barely exchanged ten sentences amongst each other Eisenhardt. I would appreciate it if your focus remained on the task at hand." His face turned red with frightening speed. Which of course seemed quite amusing to her. "Yes. Yes, of course. I take it that the reason for you bringing us here is to begin discussing our plan of action towards building the Vedrivisr." He said. "I thought that was quite clear when we left the lake." She replied. And she was right. "Uh yes. Just taking it into account once again." He said. "Yes, yes, consider it taken, I do very much wish to discuss our steps forward. As you know, Master Cray crafted this partnership on the basis of my knowledge and your ability to practically employ said knowledge in regards to finding the components to build the compass." She said, "And for that, we must of course, traverse the Stormjewel Isles, the danger of which I am sure you are already aware of." And he was, as almost all children of Kenterbury were, well versed with the dangers of that chain of islands which were a vortex of craggy cliffs and mystical energies left behind by the supposed battle of ancient sea gods.

"I'm familiar. My knowledge of the matter is that the components we require from the Isles syphon the mystical energies of the sea gods to direct our way to Valda." said William. "Precisely," She said "There lie two components or fragments rather within the southernmost and northernmost sections of the Isles, a needle, broken from what was said to be a piece of the ancient sea gods weaponry and an energy pyramid, a shard of one of those gods' very hearts, that when inserted into the framework of the Vedrivisr, provide it with power and direction, to of course, further the expedition East." The pair seemed to get along quite well when it came to discussing their passions for the great journey. As they spoke by the flickering candle flame into the night, the unfamiliarities that existed between the two began to fade ever so slightly, as they understood their own desires of how much the journey mattered to them. Unfortunately, her attitude stayed fairly unchanged. "Of course, during our expedition you will work under my command. Follow my lead. Given my superior knowledge and experience, naturally, that responsibility falls to me." She said. "Miss Freyr, for the last time out of all the politeness that still exists between us, I am not your subordinate. I am more than capable of handling some of these tasks on my own." She stared at him for a few seconds, perhaps in surprise of the fact that this was perhaps the first time he chose to assert himself in any margin, regardless of how slight.

"Fine then. During our expedition, I will guide you through with my knowledge, and any task of significant physical strain, of which there will be many of course, you can handle. You seem well equipped anyways." She said as her gaze drifted for a moment to his shoulders and down to his arms, as he caught her with his own, forcing a stalemate between their eyes as they locked for a second, arriving at some strange mutual agreement. "That's fine by me too. Any idea on how we're getting there? Belehrad is unforgiving and a boat would suffer a heavy toll against its tides." said William. "The Stormjewel Isles are only the entrance to Belehrad. The sea should permit passage by boat to them, and given we manage with a degree of care, the boat itself should be fine to carry us back as well. Any manner of actual danger lies within the Isles themselves." said Ilsa.

"The storm is dangerous, yes, but given a degree of steadfastness and care, and of course, travelling under cover, they shouldn't pose that great of a risk, should they?" asked William, under the assumption of the fact that any real danger she spoke of was only of the harsh weather that gave the Isles their namesake. And for a moment that sense of unfamiliarity crept back between the two once again. Ilsa stared at him with a look of analytical confusion once again as she spoke "Eisenhardt, you're either incredibly naive or still oblivious of the information that the storm is the least of our concerns within those Isles. Do you really think our company is the only one in search of what it takes to build the Vedrivisr? How much has Master Cray really kept from you?" The sense of internal frustration that lay dormant within William had now escaped its chambers and was beginning to boil within the boy, one that was fuelled by his lack of understanding as to why Cray had kept information of such significance from him, which until now had served as the primary reason as to why he seemed so very lost during almost every interaction with his partner so far. Their next meeting would certainly see the voicing of these concerns in a fairly vocal manner, he thought. But he knew also that, in the grand scheme of things, this expedition would be paramount to the journey. And so his complaints went suppressed for now.

She continued however, much to William's dismay as his lack of knowledge of the matter began to weigh on him quite heavily now, as what she spoke of next was of significant concern. "The Ministry of Foreign Affairs in our town is an extension of the Crown's authority, Eisenhardt, of the Arianorian High Court. And while they use this branch as a method to obtain relics of importance to the journey East, so do their enemies." She said, intriguing the boy, who truly was quite oblivious to any matters of the sort. "Enemies? Enemies of the Crown? Which of those exist within The Glades?

Her face grew dimmer, and it was almost as though the green in her eyes dimmed to a dark grey, unreasonable as it sounded. "Agents of the North. Of Rykaria. The rebellion still continues Eisenhardt, and you should know that Valda holds great prospects not only for the Crown, but also for those seeking to tear it down." She said, to which he replied- "Rykaria? But the North was crushed during King Surton's time when the Frostlord was defeated. How is it th-", "Yes, and that's the story that every man, woman and child believes by word of the Crown, a pretence that exists so the Crown Regent can keep the continent away from the continued existence of the Northern Rebellion. King Surton's victory over the Frostlord kept them at bay for a long while, but never extinguished them. And now they rise again. Do you really think the quest for Valda exists only to claim treasures and take a gander at the views, Eisenhardt?" said Ilsa.

William was shocked but absorbed the impact of this information relatively fast, keeping in mind now the true urgency of this mission. "So you're saying we're dealing with the storm coupled with Rykarian operatives in the Isles as well? Therefore making me the brawn of this operation and you the brain. I see now," He said, "Finally, we reach some common ground. It was not till now that I had the faintest idea of this danger, and I will equip myself accordingly then. Then we can't waste anymore time. I'm leaving to prepare, and I'm guessing our plans fall in line."

She stared at him with that face again that seemed as if she was taking a measure of him, except this time, William didn't shy away from questioning why, "You do that quite often do you not? Analyse me? Ever since the lake it feels as though you've been compiling a judgement of me Miss Freyr. Would it be overly rude to ask why?"

And she was stunned now, so to speak, or at the very least upon the basis of what her face let off. The light flickered ever dimmer now, close to fading, as he got up, lamp by his waist, but yet in wait for her answer. And she spoke then, after almost completely masking the initial surprise of what seemed like a fairly bold move from William, taking into account his presentation of himself so far, "It isn't far from ordinary to take an account of the person who's planning on serving as your accompaniment to an island covered in storms and foreign spies, especially considering this being a person you met about only 3 hours ago. And as far as judgements go, haven't you been quite attentive as well? Your gaze certainly says so, Eisenhardt."

He wasn't planning on getting caught off guard by that manoeuvre this time around, despite his continued failure at hiding the redness within his cheeks, "A person you met 3 hours ago Miss Freyr, and by my knowledge, might have known about for far longer than 3 months. Given your experience, of course. Or is that assessment of mine incorrect?" The silence that followed made a little pocket for itself within that corner of the jolly tavern, and was long enough for the candle to flicker out entirely. She got up, wearing her cloak once more and sinking into it once more, as she spoke "Perhaps my judgement of you is changing even at this very moment, but I suppose both of us should most certainly focus on the task at hand above all else right now, yes?" She said as she pulled the cloaks over her head, masking her locks, with the slightest hint of a one sided smile underneath, "We meet at Velnar Beach tomorrow at sundown. There's a boat there, fit for two, and ready to take us to the Southern island of the Stormjewel Isles. I hope punctuality serves some importance to you, especially now that you understand the stakes at play here."

The dimness of the corner that they were in seemed also to dim the noise of the tavern as the only light they saw was that which passed through their eyes as they looked at each other once again, in complete seriousness now understanding the nature of the expedition. "I'll be there. The day will allow me to gain perhaps a few answers from Master Cray as well." said William. "Sure. But I should say again that I'm equally as oblivious as to why he would keep matters of such importance from you. Considering it's quite unlike him to mask any information of the sort, maybe it would be interesting for me to know too." she replied. "And what exactly is it that you know already? If I may ask of course, since beyond my name it would appear you seem to possess some knowledge of who I am despite our first meeting being...today night?"

he said. "Well, you may most certainly ask, but after we've got that compass, yes? I believe that to be a fair condition." She said, despite William's firm belief that it was in no way a fair condition whatsoever, considering he rightfully had every justification to learn as to why she knew about him in the first place. Thoughts of which none were vocalised.

And so he led her outside the tavern, bustling ever still, but with the drunkards having settled down, seeing as they might just have pushed their livers to the tipping point. The sun gleamed on the horizon and painted the sky as though it were its personal canvas, in all manner of different hues, shining a gradient across the clouds, as the moonless night dissipated now, with the two stepping out, as they looked at each other again before parting ways while she walked eastward and William west, to the Ministry now, where on the way back, their thoughts were divided into two. The Isles being the first fraction, and the other being, each other, as they began now to wonder about how each one thought of the other, and what a strange meeting this was indeed. And what perils may await these newfound companions in their journey forward, and what this would mean for them. For it was so that lightning flashed now on the other end of the horizon, signalling the mystical vortex that their journey would lead them to.

Notes of Importance

Places of Importance

Kenterbury - Southeastern port town, where the primary story takes place. Residence of the Eisenhardts and Freyrs, and current centre of focus of the capital's expansion of the Eastward Ships.

The Greet of Silence - Ancestral home of the Eisenhardt stonemasons, within the far corner of Kenterbury.

Valda - Vast eastern continent to the land of Arendor, much of which is yet unexplored, but is said to hold no small number of mystical wonders.

Arendor - Great western continent, and home of the Arianorians.

Arianor - Capital city of the Crownlands, namesake of the Arianorians, home to the King, or any governing figure of the land.

The Crownlands - Sacred land to the Arianorians, claimed by the First King of Arianor, Arfin, and under the capital's rule.

Magistrate of Foreign Affairs - A name given to the office building of the Head of Mystical Exploration, which was previously the Ministry of Foreign Affairs before its recent renovation.

Erfenia - Southern section of the continent of Arendor

Inarion - Western land of Erfenia, home to lesser kings and ealdormen.

Fae Gyora - Southern land of Erfenia, land closest to what many consider the edge of the world, residence of merchants and traders.

The Glades - Eastern land of Erfenia, within which is the town of Kenturbury to the very eastern sea.

Erenheldor - Northern land of Erfenia, considered a sister region to The Crownlands, also mostly under rule of the Crown, and following many of its sentiments.

Gulf of Vedrinoldr - Entrance to the eastern sea leading to Valda, next to Kenterbury, within which lie the Stormjewel Isles.

Rykaria - Harsh fractured land to the north of Arendor, breeding ground to many rebellions against the crown, and home of petty lords and dark sorcerers.

Holfingr - Capital city of Rykaria and base of operations for the Frostlord of Holfingr prior to his defeat in the War of Winter.

Belehrad - Great Eastern sea of terrible storms separating Arendor and Valda.

Lake of Zephyr - Lake on the outskirts of Kenterbury, within the east of The Glades, known for its particularly strong gusts of wind and breeze.

Antler's Rest - Tavern on the northwestern border of Kenterbury.

Velnar Beach - A beach of relatively small size towards the north of Kenterbury, grazing its borders, while remaining quite remote.

People of importance

William Eisenhardt - Eager explorer of a tender age and the youngest of the Eisenhardt family, working as an apprentice of Syrion Cray for the Magistrate of Foreign Affairs.

Ilsa Freyr - Mysterious partner of William Eisenhardt on his mission to the Stormjewel Isles, also working for the Magistrate of Foreign Affairs.

Erik Eisenhardt - Chief stonemason of Kenterbury, and currently the eldest within the Eisenhardt family, exempting the existence of Volnar Eisenhardt, his father, who remains missing following his journey to Inarion. Father of William Eisenhardt.

Syrion Cray - Acting Head of Mystical Exploration within Kenterbury, as appointed by the Crown and Master of William Eisenhardt.

Gordolfen Galandor - Current head of the Galandor bloodline and Crown Regent of Arianor, also known as Gordolfen the Glutton.

King Surton I - Legendary King of Arianor, First of his name and wilder of the Crimson Blade of Imladrion.

Imladrion - Ancient Arendorian deity of fire, volcanos and purification.

Frostlord of Holfingr - Rival to King Surton and leader of the Rykarian rebellions, practitioner of the highest level of Frost magics.

Follow the light of the moon in Volume 2: Vortex of Frost